Good-bye, Chicken Little

Good-bye, Chicken Little

BETSY BYARS

HarperTrophy®
A Division of HarperCollinsPublishers

Harper Trophy® is a registered trademark of
HarperCollins Publishers, Inc.

Library of Congress Cataloging-in-Publication Data
Byars, Betsy Cromer.
  Good-bye, Chicken Little.

  Summary: A boy discovers that he doesn't have to feel
personally responsible for his uncle's drowning.
  [1. Death—Fiction.   2. Family life—Fiction]
I. Title.
PZ7.B9836Gp   1979   [Fic]   78-19829
ISBN 0-06-020907-0
ISBN 0-06-020911-9 (lib. bdg.)
ISBN 0-06-440291-6 (pbk.)

First Harper Trophy edition, 1990.

Good-bye, Chicken Little

one

Four days before Christmas, Jimmie Little's uncle announced he would walk across the Monday River. It was a sudden decision, made after several beers in Harry's Bar and Grill, and at once the other customers, posse-like, hurried him to the riverbank.

Up the hill, in his house, Jimmie Little was standing by the clothes drier, waiting for his jeans to dry. Suddenly the kitchen door burst open.

Jimmie spun around. "Will you close that door? I am standing here in my underwear."

"Your uncle's getting ready to walk across the Monday River!" his friend Conrad shouted. He was panting for breath.

It was Conrad who brought Jimmie most of his bad news, and all of it in a loud, excited and—it seemed to Jimmie—happy voice.

"What?" Jimmie asked. He put one hand on the drier for support. The drier was so old that it trembled with every rotation.

"Come *on*! Some men in Harry's Bar and Grill bet your uncle he couldn't walk across the river and he's going to try."

"But the ice is too thin. He'll fall through."

"*You* know that. *I* know that. The men at *Harry's* know that. But your uncle—" With both hands he made circular motions around his head to indicate that Uncle Pete was a little lacking in that area.

"Come on!" he urged.

Jimmie took his jeans from the drier and pulled them on. The seams were still damp.

"Come *on*!" Conrad pressed Jimmie's jacket and cap into his hands.

Jimmie grimaced, not only because of the discomfort of the damp jeans. He would have wanted to go down to the river and watch somebody else's uncle try to walk across. Lately, however, he had begun to notice that his own family drew attention to themselves in the wrong way. They did silly, senseless things that made them look foolish even when they succeeded.

He put on his jacket and drew his stocking cap on his head. Then he followed Conrad out the door, dragging his feet along as if they were the heaviest part of his body.

"Hurry!" Conrad urged. "If we miss this . . ."

"I'm hurrying as fast as I can," Jimmie said.

As they picked up speed, Conrad began going over Uncle Pete's chances. "He *could* make it. It *could* be solid. On the other hand, I have to admit it looks thin out in the middle, Jimbo."

Jimmie glanced at Conrad and then away. Conrad was always giving people nicknames, but he took great pleasure in his own name, Conrad Pugh, and forbade anyone to call him Connie.

"It's a football player's name," he had once told Jimmie enthusiastically. "With a name like Conrad Pugh, I got to be one of the all-time greats." And so, based only on a name odd enough to rank with Haven Moses and Claudie Minor, he had chosen his life's occupation.

As they rounded the curve they saw the river. "Yeah, Jimbo, it does look thin," Conrad said.

The ice was pale green, streaked with white patches of blown snow. On the bank a group of people had gathered, mostly men and children. "Not as big a crowd as Billy Carter got when he opened the Mall," Conrad commented.

"No," Jimmie agreed. He pulled his jacket collar up against the wind.

Winter had come early this year. Usually it was January, with its bitter storms, when the river froze. But now, four days before Christmas, the river was, or appeared to be, frozen solid.

"Hey, Jimmie," a boy in the crowd yelled, "your uncle's going across!"

"I know," he answered in a voice too low to be heard.

He sighed inwardly. For the first time in his life he regretted the holidays. He wanted all his friends to be in school. He even wanted to be there himself, stumbling over a lesson or opening his peanut-butter-and-bologna sandwich in the cafeteria.

"Hey, we're in luck. Your uncle hasn't started yet," Conrad said.

"Yes, that's luck all right."

Uncle Pete was standing with the men from Harry's Bar and Grill. Two of the men, partially sobered by the frigid air, were trying to talk him out of the attempt. Uncle Pete laughed and shook his head. He was a man who, all his life, had tried anything. Someone had only to say "Nobody can . . ." or "I bet you can't . . ." and he would be off.

"Uncle Pete," Jimmie said, "what are you getting ready to do?"

His uncle turned. His face was red from the cold and the beer. He wore a checkered cap and matching scarf.

"I'm going to take a walk," Uncle Pete said. "And don't you tell your mother." His breath turned the cold air to steam.

"Hopefully a dry walk," one of the men said. The others laughed.

"Uncle Pete—"

"I have wanted to do this all my life." Uncle Pete threw his scarf about his neck in a gallant, old-timey gesture. "That river has been waiting for someone to walk across it for a hundred years."

"But listen—"

"I grew up hearing it was impossible to walk across that river, and I'm surprised it took me this long to try."

He turned quickly and slid down the bank. He got to his feet, laughing, and turned. "I want to get all my falling out of the way before I hit the ice."

"*Hit* may be just the right word."

Uncle Pete, feigning fear, took a few steps out on the ice. It was like the comedy routines at Ice Capades when someone from the audience steps on the ice and pretends to be unsteady.

"You'll get your ice legs in a minute," one of the men called.

Up on the sidewalk a group of children from the Baptist kindergarten paused to watch.

"Boys and girls, keep walking. It's too cold to stop," their teacher said.

They stood without moving, in twos, holding hands tightly. The first thing they had learned in kindergarten was the buddy system.

"We want to *see*," a boy in a Yogi Bear face mask protested.

"Yes, we want to *see*," cried the class echo.

"Now, boys and girls, we don't want to be late for *Santa Claus*, do we?" The teacher leaned toward them. "We told Santa we'd be at the Mall at one o'clock!"

But their faces were turned to the pale green of the Monday River, and the lone figure starting across the ice. Even Santa with his promises of gifts somehow paled beside that figure.

"Well, five minutes," the teacher conceded, then added as an afterthought, "but do *we* ever walk on ice, boys and girls?"

"No, Miss Elizabeth."

"Why?"

"Because we might fall through!"

This childish recitation sent a chill to Jimmie's bones. "Why does he do these things?" Jimmie asked.

"It's just the way he is," Conrad explained. "And let's face it, he may make it, get his picture in the paper, be a hero!"

Uncle Pete picked up a stick from the ice. He pretended to be an old man, broken by age, picking his

6

way over the ice. The men laughed. Encouraged, Uncle Pete suddenly turned into Charlie Chaplin. Cane swinging, he walked comically on the green ice.

Jimmie clamped his legs together. The seams of his pants were frozen. His legs were beginning to tremble. In his jacket pockets, he crossed his fingers for luck.

two

"Actually, your family's always doing crazy stuff," Conrad said.

There was no point in Jimmie's denying it with Uncle Pete ten feet out onto the Monday River. Uncle Pete was now crouched down like a football player. He ran forward, turned and caught an imaginary ball. The crowd on the riverbank cheered.

There were cheers from the bridge too, and Conrad punched Jimmie. He pointed to the people leaning over the rail. "Crowd's growing."

Jimmie nodded.

Conrad glanced at him. "Except you. You don't do much crazy stuff."

Jimmie felt grateful for being excluded, even momentarily, from his crazy family.

8

"Maybe you'll get that way though, when you're older. Maybe it'll come out later—you know, like a beard."

"Maybe."

Jimmie kept watching his uncle. Uncle Pete had paused twenty feet out on the ice to call back, "Solid as a rock." Then he began moving again, sliding his feet forward in an imitation skating movement.

"Way to go," one of the men called. He had a ten-dollar bet that Uncle Pete would make it.

"Course you did do one crazy thing," Conrad admitted.

Jimmie did not ask what this crazy thing was because he didn't want to hear about it. He glanced at Conrad, his look telling him to shut up, and then turned back to Uncle Pete.

Uncle Pete had one arm in front, one in back. He was singing, "La, la-da da deeeeee," as he skated forward in his brown oxfords.

"I'm talking about the time you got the turkey bone in your foot."

"That was an accident."

"Sure, but with anybody else it would have been a splinter or a plain piece of glass. I mean, how many people in the world, in the whole world, do you think step on a turkey bone and have to go to the hospital to have it removed?"

"Just me."

"That's my point." He lowered his voice for privacy. "You know, one time I did something *sort of* crazy. I never told this to anybody."

Jimmie said nothing. He knew Conrad had told him, at one time or another, every single thing that had ever happened to him. The secret things, the things Conrad claimed he had never told anybody, Jimmie knew well enough to recite along with him.

"Of course, I was little, three or four, and didn't know any better. But anyway, I was out in the backyard, and all of a sudden I stuck a rock up my nose. To this day I don't know why I did it, Jimbo. I surprised myself. I went in the house boo-hooing, 'There's a rock up my nose! There's a rock up my nose!'"

Conrad was dividing his interest between his story and Uncle Pete. His eyes darted from Uncle Pete to Jimmie's face.

"Well, my mom wanted to take me to the doctor because there's a special instrument for getting rocks out of kids' noses. It's painless. Only my dad said no. He said if she took me to the doctor, I'd keep on sticking rocks up my nose, just to be taken to the doctor." Conrad now devoted himself completely to his story. "Like going to the doctor was a treat!"

Uncle Pete was thirty feet onto the ice now, still

skating. He paused to call back, "Would anybody care to see me do a triple toe loop?"

"I'd like to see that triple toe loop, Pete," a man called.

Uncle Pete lifted his toe and made three tiny loops in the air. As he started forward, Conrad picked up his story.

"Anyway, so my Dad said he'd get the rock out himself—and my dad is not a gentle man, Jimmie. And after he got it out he told me if I ever put another rock up my nose, he'd put a *fist* up my nose, and after that, well, somehow, Jimbo, I just never particularly wanted to put another rock up my nose. I mean, let's face it—"

On the ice Uncle Pete stopped skating. He stood still for a moment. The men from Harry's had smiles on their faces, waiting to see what funny thing Uncle Pete would do now.

"Something's wrong," Jimmie said.

Uncle Pete took another step forward. He was moving slowly now, looking down at the ice as if he had lost something.

"He's getting ready to say something funny," Conrad predicted.

"No, something's wrong."

Uncle Pete was a hundred feet out on the ice now, approaching the middle of the river. Here the chan-

11

nel was deep. The water below the ice was swift. This was the most dangerous part.

Uncle Pete reached out with his right foot and tested the ice in front of him. He took another step. He eased his left foot forward. He was moving with the caution of a tightrope walker, only it was not an imitation.

The ice cracked loudly. The sound was as sharp as a rifle shot, and the crowd got silent. The smiles on the men's faces faded. Conrad drew in his breath and held it.

"Come on back," Jimmie yelled. He ran forward a few steps. He slid down the bank, his pants catching on the frozen broom grass. He skidded onto the ice.

The river was cold and merciless in the winter. The wind that blew between the banks was sharp enough to cut through any cloth. Jimmie wrapped his arms around himself.

"Come back!"

"Run for it!" a man behind Jimmie yelled.

Uncle Pete stood with his back to them. His legs were apart, his arms stretched out to the side as if for balance. Only the ends of the scarf, caught in the wind, flapped around his neck.

No one on the bank spoke. Above them, on the bridge, that crowd had grown silent. Beyond, on the west bank, workers on lunch break from the glass factory had gathered and stood motionless too.

It was a moment in time that couldn't be measured in minutes and seconds. Everything in the world seemed to have stopped.

Slowly Uncle Pete began to turn. His arms were still stretched out to the side. Like a figure on a music box, he seemed to be turning without any footwork.

There was another cracking sound from the ice.

"*Run* for it!" the man urged again. He stumbled down the bank. *"Run!"*

The ice cracked a third time, and Uncle Pete started toward them. Jimmie closed his eyes.

It was an instinct he had acquired when he was little—to close his eyes when there was something he could not bear to see. In this way he had avoided seeing his dog Fritzie hit by a truck and his father's body brought out of the coal mine.

Eyes squeezed shut, he heard the scream of the crowd. It was such a unified, unearthly cry that there was no question what had caused it.

He opened his eyes and saw the hole in the ice. It was a small jagged hole, and Jimmie could not believe that Uncle Pete could have disappeared into a hole that small.

His eyes scanned the ice to see if Uncle Pete had, at the last minute, somehow miraculously made his

13

escape. He half expected to see him clowning like Charlie Chaplin on the far bank.

Then he looked again at the dark hole in the ice. The convincing detail was Uncle Pete's checkered cap, which lay just beside the hole.

Some of the men ran down the bank and onto the ice. Then they came to a helpless stop. "He didn't even struggle," one said.

"He didn't even yell."

"He should have run for it!" another said, striking his fist into his hand.

"What happened?" Jimmie asked. He turned to Conrad, whose face, beneath his Steeler stocking cap, was stricken.

"He went down," Conrad said.

Jimmie reached out and grabbed Conrad by the arms. "But how?" He had avoided seeing it, but now it was terribly important that he understand it. "I've got to know what happened!"

"He just went down," Conrad said again. He extended his hands in a gesture of his own helplessness.

"But *how*?"

"It was so quick I just—" Conrad shook his head. "It was—I don't know—he just went down!"

Jimmie turned his eyes back to the hole in the ice, the cap.

Up on the sidewalk, the teacher was rushing the

kindergarten children back up the hill. "I'll tell you later," she said again and again to their shrill questions.

As the childish cries faded into the distance, an awful adult silence came over the crowd by the Monday River.

They stood without moving, frozen in place, as if they were on a stage waiting for directions. They stood exactly as they were until a man on the bridge, using his CB radio, called the police.

three

"Do you suppose," Jimmie asked slowly, picking his words carefully, "that Uncle Pete could have fallen *into* the river, *under* the ice, and then—" He paused as he got to the important part. "And then he could have come up farther down the river?"

Conrad shook his head.

"It *could* happen."

Conrad was still shaking his head. "Not in real life."

Jimmie nodded. They had both already sensed the difference between a fictional world where miracles depended on a writer's imagination and the real world where a harsh, unimaginative law ruled.

They paused on the back porch of Jimmie's house. Jimmie's nose was running, but he had not noticed.

"You want me to come in with you?" Conrad asked. He wiped his own dry nose and sniffed loudly.

Jimmie shook his head.

"Your mom must be home now. I hear her sewing machine."

"Yes."

"You're *sure* you don't want me to come in with you?" Conrad asked. He was torn between a desire to help his friend and the need to be in his own tragedy-free home. He felt he wanted to watch one of those cartoons where characters who fall through the ice are safe in the next frame, plotting more mischief.

Also he knew he would have wanted, would have insisted on, Jimmie coming in with him. "I can't do it alone" was one of his favorite expressions.

"No." Jimmie opened the door and entered.

"I'll wait," Conrad called. "You may want me." He sat down on the top step and began jiggling his legs to keep warm.

In the kitchen it seemed to Jimmie that the whole house had changed. There was a strange emptiness. Even the hum of his mother's sewing machine in the next room had a different, unnatural sound.

"Mom?"

"Hmmmm," she called back.

He walked into the bedroom. She looked up, a

17

pleased expression on her face. She loved to make her own clothes. It was the only way she could be sure no one else would have the same outfit.

"*You* can look like everybody in the world, if you want to," she told her best friend, Polly, who bought her clothes at Murphy's Mart. "Me, I don't want to bump into myself coming and going." Polly had glanced at her latest outfit, a flapping, beltless dress of green drapery material, and admitted that was unlikely.

Because her mouth was filled with pins, she gave a sound of interest. "Hmmmm?" It was a question.

She slid a pin from her sewing into her mouth with the others. She eased the cloth around a difficult seam and snipped a thread.

"Uncle Pete fell in the river," he blurted out. "I think he drowned."

There was a total terrible silence, and then the sound of pins falling onto the wooden surface of the machine as she opened her mouth. "What?" The pins rained from the machine to the floor.

"He was trying to walk across the river and he fell in." Jimmie was stuttering, shivering as hard as if he had fallen into the river too. He tried to wipe his nose on his jacket sleeve. "I think he drowned."

His mother got up slowly, heavily. She valued her family. No matter how old or wild or crazy or

18

troublesome—she prized them.

She brushed past Jimmie. In the living room she threw her coat over her shoulders.

"Mom, there's nothing you can do."

With her coat flaring out behind her like a cape, she went out the back door. Conrad leaped to his feet and down the steps just in time to let her pass.

"Mom!" Jimmie called, but she did not hear him.

Without speaking again, Jimmie followed her down the hill. He was not trying to catch up with her, just to keep her in sight. Behind him, like a detached shadow, came Conrad.

Mrs. Little was the picture of distress and tragedy as she ran to the river. She stood on the bank, her hands to her eyes, and looked over the pale-green sheet of ice. As she saw the small jagged hole where Uncle Pete had disappeared, the cap beside it, her hands fell and covered her heart.

There were three women and two policemen there, and they gathered around her. Jimmie saw that nothing they said comforted her. Indeed, she held out her hands as if to ward off their comfort.

It was, Jimmie thought, a pantomime of grief. His mother wrapped her arms around her body. She swirled and clasped her hands to her head. She turned to demand something of the tall policeman, and then fell to the ground, her coat still flaring out behind her. Her bright-red coat was the only spot of color on the scene.

The three women got her to her feet and began to walk her up the hill. Jimmie stood waiting with his hands in his pockets. He felt as sick as if he had a disease.

"They'll find the body," one of the women was saying as they approached Jimmie and Conrad. This was a coal-mining community, and bringing bodies out after a coal-mine disaster was important.

Mrs. Little shook her head. She did not even hear the woman.

Pete, her younger brother, had been her favorite. She had raised him like a pet. "You clown," she was always saying to him, and the way she said it made it the highest compliment. Her face was crumpled now. She looked her age. Yet at the same time there was something young and disbelieving about her eyes.

"Why didn't they stop him?" she asked the women. She tossed her head in misery and caught sight of Jimmie. "Why didn't they stop him?" she asked.

He opened his mouth to answer, but she stopped him with another question.

"Why didn't *you* stop him?"

He was stunned by the question and the suddenly hard look in her damp eyes.

20

"Were you there?" she asked. She shook off the women's hands and moved one step closer to Jimmie.

"Yes."

"You should have stopped him!"

"I tried to, Mom. I told him not to do it," he stammered.

"You should have *stopped* him!"

"He really did try," Conrad chimed in. His voice was too weak to be his own.

Mrs. Little's eyes, on Jimmie, flicked over to include Conrad in her accusation. He stepped back.

"Jimmie, he was *family*!" she cried.

He nodded.

His mother considered every member of her family unique, an individual who had never been on this earth before and never would be again. The family was like a great tasty recipe, and the loss of any member made it less spicy, less enjoyable.

Jimmie looked down at his feet. He could feel that his mother was still watching him with her hard, unblinking eyes.

One of the women said, "Come on, Mrs. Little," in a soothing voice, but she would not be moved.

"Mom, he was a grown man," he said, looking up at her.

"He was many, many things," she said. Tears were rolling down her cheeks now. "But he was never a

21

grown man."

"Now, Mrs. Little, you're going to make yourself sick. Come on in—"

"He was a *boy*!" She made an explosion of the word. "And if someone is a *boy*—I don't care how old he is in age—if someone is a *boy*, then you stop him from doing things that will hurt him. Do you understand me?"

He thought for a moment that she was going to reach out and strike him, something she had never done before in all his life.

"I understand," he said. He spoke so softly he wasn't sure his mother had heard him.

He saw his uncle at Halloween, hilariously done up in one of his mother's outfits, trick-or-treating the neighbors. He saw his uncle in Mike's Diner, clowning, pretending to the waitress that he spoke only Hungarian. He saw his uncle at the table, his chair tilted to the wall, his cap pushed back on his head, telling of some joke he had pulled, some trick he had played. He saw his uncle ice-skating across the Monday River to his death.

He felt tears sting his eyes. He sighed.

His mother turned away as if she had been waiting for that sigh. Slowly, accepting the women's help now, she began walking up the hill.

One of the women tucked her coat collar closer

about her neck. As the three women entered the backyard of the house, Mrs. Little began to shake her head from side to side, slowly, as if she refused to accept that this had happened.

Jimmie kept standing where he was, his hands stuck in his pockets.

"For what it's worth," Conrad said, "I don't think you could have stopped him."

Jimmie drew up his shoulders and let them fall.

"Do *you* think you could have stopped him?"

Again, Jimmie shrugged. He felt as if he'd just been put on a huge, complex scale, and he was too small and inexperienced to read the numbers.

"I don't know," he said.

four

"Well, I better go," Conrad said finally.

Jimmie nodded. They separated, and Jimmie started up the hill alone. At the Bakers' driveway he stopped. He realized he could not go into his house and see his mother again. Yet he knew he could not walk past the river either. That river would never be just scenery to him again. He was trapped here at the Bakers' driveway.

He felt strange. As soon as his mother had called Uncle Pete a boy, he had found that he himself no longer felt like a boy. He was not a man yet, he knew that, but something vital, something important about boyhood, had been taken away from him with his mother's words. He wasn't sure he would get it back.

It was, he decided, as if he had all of a sudden

grown up without getting any adult skills or adult knowledge.

He walked over and sat heavily on the Bakers' sagging porch steps. The Bakers' house was the worst in the neighborhood. Bricks had fallen from the chimney and still lay where they had fallen. Shingles on the roof blew away in a hard wind. But now the house had been decorated with fifty-two strings of outdoor Christmas lights that glowed day and night. Every peeling window frame, every door, every rotting column, every stunted bush, had been outlined. Jimmie sat down in the midst of the bright twinkling lights. He closed his eyes.

When he was younger, the year his father was killed in the coal mine, he became overwhelmed with fear. It seemed to him then that there were scary headlines everywhere—seventy-eight killed here, eleven there, a Boy Scout running to join his campmates was struck by lightning, a plane crash killed 112, a flash flood took a whole trailer court.

And Jimmie could see no reason to it. It was as if some impish gods had got hold of the earth and for diversion made planes fall and coal mines collapse. He didn't see how his mother, his sister, went about life as usual—crossing streets in the middle of the block, sleeping through thunderstorms.

Without his father, he felt completely unprotected.

25

He was like a snail turned out of its shell. His anxiety became so great that at one point he began calling himself Chicken Little.

"Oh, come on," Conrad would say, "it's going to be a nonviolent battle—just you and me and Parotti against the Fletcher brothers."

"Look, this is *me* you're talking to—Chicken Little," he would say, making a joke of his fear.

Or, "Come on, Jimbo, let's race across the railroad trestle. There's not a train in sight."

"Chicken Little doesn't race across railroad trestles," he would answer.

Sometimes he would be too chicken not to take part, and he would actually find himself fighting one of the Fletcher brothers or racing across the railroad trestle in a fit of fear that left him physically ill. It was a constant source of amazement to him that everyone continued to think he was not really afraid, just being funny.

Later, during the summer of that awful year, he began to think he had said good-bye to Chicken Little. Fear no longer turned his legs weak. Danger no longer seemed to hover just outside his bedroom window at night.

But now Jimmie saw that was not true. Chicken Little had been there all the time, just waiting to swoop in upon him like Peter Pan.

"Jimmie!"

He looked up. At the top of the hill one of the women was calling him. She beckoned from his back door.

"Your mother wants you!"

Slowly, eyes to the ground, he started up the hill. As he walked, he went back over that moment just before Uncle Pete had stepped out onto the ice. He tried to remember exactly what he had said to Uncle Pete. Had he actually, really, tried to stop Uncle Pete, or had it been like that time at Conrad's house when Bucky Harris had insisted on making an anonymous call to the principal, and Conrad, eyes shining, had said, "If he wants to, Jimbo, *let* him!"

But what he had actually said and done was blanked out by what had happened. All he could remember clearly—and this he knew he would never forget—was the shape of that dark jagged hole in the ice, the round cap beside it.

He opened the door and went into the living room, where his mother was sitting, her face turned to their Christmas tree. They made their own ornaments—it was part of his mother's enjoyment of things that were different. Now, however, her eyes didn't focus on the ornaments.

"Jimmie." She looked at him. Her eyes were soft now, motherly. "Come here." She took one of his

27

hands and held it between hers. "I am really sorry for what I said out there."

"That's all right."

"I didn't even know what I was saying."

"It's all right."

It occurred to him that perhaps the reason birds and animals communicated so well was because they didn't have words to confuse matters. They had their sniffs and scents and sounds that meant one specific thing.

"There is no way that you could have stopped Pete if he wanted to walk across the river. I know how determined he could be. I was just terribly, terribly upset."

"I know that."

"If I blame anyone it's those men at Harry's, not you." She was looking at him so intently that he wanted to turn away. "You are in no way to blame." She pronounced each word separately.

He nodded.

She gave him a sad smile. "Then it's forgotten?"

"Yes."

The phone rang, and his mother jumped to her feet. "That must be Helena." With her coat still around her shoulders, she hurried into the kitchen to answer it.

In her haste she bumped into the table and grabbed the stove for support. She moved awkwardly when she was upset. It was as if the world had shriveled out of shape, leaving her too big for her surroundings.

"Oh, *Conrad*," she said in a disappointed voice. Then, "Yes, you can talk to him for a minute, but I'm expecting a call."

Jimmie took the phone from his mother. "Hello."

Conrad was slightly out of breath because he had run all the way home to call Jimmie. When they had parted, Conrad had felt as if he was sending Jimmie to some dreadful fate. He still remembered the look on Mrs. Little's face. It had been as awesome and terrible as something in a dramatic production.

"Is everything all right?" he asked.

"Yes."

"Look, do you want to go to the Mall with me? I haven't done my Christmas shopping yet."

"I can't."

"It won't take long. I know exactly what I'm going to get." He began to tick off his choices. "Gardenia cologne for my mom, scented notepaper for my sister—"

"I have to stay here," Jimmie interrupted.

"Come on, it'll be good for you to get out." Conrad felt as if he was making an important rescue.

"Jimmie," his mother warned in the doorway.

"I've got to go."

Jimmie hung up the phone, but he continued to

stand by the window. The winter sun shone through the icy panes. Jimmie's mother believed there was special power in the winter sun—this was why dogs and cats, sensing something beyond human knowledge, lay in it at every opportunity. Jimmie moved closer to the healing rays.

As he looked out the window he saw his sister, Cassie, coming up the hill. She was saying something to her boyfriend, laughing out loud, so Jimmie knew she had not heard the news about Uncle Pete.

"I can tell you exactly what I'm giving you for Christmas," Cassie was saying. "Nothing!"

"Come on, Cassie, what are you giving me really?"

They were on the back porch now. Roger was leaning against the door, blocking her way.

"Why do you want to know?" Cassie asked. "So you'll know how much to spend on me?"

"No."

"That's it, isn't it? All right, if you must know, I spent forty-nine cents."

"Forty-nine cents! What can you get for forty-nine cents? Even a T-shirt costs—"

"I got you two goldfish."

"Goldfish! Cassie, did you get me *goldfish*?"

Roger was still leaning against the door, waiting for Cassie's answer, when Mrs. Little jerked the door open. He stumbled backward into the kitchen, a foolish smile dying on his face.

"Pete's dead," Mrs. Little told Cassie.

"Uncle Pete?"

Mrs. Little nodded. As she began to tell the story, she burst into tears again. Roger straightened. He looked helplessly at Cassie over her mother's head. "I'll call you later," he said. He backed out the door.

Mrs. Little started again. "It happened this afternoon. Pete was at Harry's Bar. The men dared him." Her voice broke after each sentence.

Jimmie turned abruptly and went to his room. He closed the door. He began to fiddle with the things on his dresser, spinning his hairbrush around like a top. All the while he listened to his mother's voice in the kitchen.

Oddly enough, he found that the talk with his mother in the living room had made him feel worse about Uncle Pete's death instead of better. There were some things you couldn't take back. They had already hit the mark, left a scar.

He continued to spin his hairbrush around, watching without interest as the handle pointed first to the picture of his father, then to his jug of pennies, then to the pain in his chest.

When his mother had told Cassie the entire story, he lay down on his bed and stared up at the ceiling.

five

"I'll have to get the car out," Mrs. Little said.

She announced this so slowly and carefully that driving the car became the once-a-year, all-important event it really was.

The car, a 1954 DeSoto, had belonged to Jimmie's grandfather and had been kept over the years as a kind of memorial to him. The DeSoto was stored in the basement garage and, for extra protection, had been covered with a layer of old blankets and quilts. When the blankets and quilts were removed and the DeSoto stood there, its chrome gleaming, its maroon finish shining, Jimmie always thought, "Wouldn't Grandpa be proud?" And he was filled with a flash of his mother's familial pride.

"What do you need the car for?" Cassie asked.

They were sitting at the supper table. No one was hungry for the meat casserole, which Mrs. Baker had sent over and which Cassie claimed had been made of Alpo.

"Now, look at that," she had said. "Real meat doesn't come in perfect little chunks like that and like that and like that." Her plate was covered with round chunks which she had picked from the casserole to prove her point.

She had been dissecting one of the cubes like a suspicious scientist when Mrs. Little made her announcement about the car. Now Cassie looked up. She was distracted for the first time from the casserole.

"I have decided," Mrs. Little said, "that I am going to have the entire family—what is left of it—over for a party."

Mrs. Little had been unnaturally quiet, in a sort of tragic slump, for the day and a half since Pete's death. Now she sat erect. She seemed miraculously cured of a fatal illness.

"A party!" Cassie cried.

"And I will need the car to go and get some of the people."

"Who?"

"Well, Uncle C. C., for one. I'll have to go for him the day before the party and—"

"Mom, you can't be serious about having Uncle C. C."

Mrs. Little gave her a look that would have silenced anyone but Cassie. Two minutes earlier it would have silenced Cassie too, but now she felt her mother was back to normal and therefore capable of an argument.

"Mom, Uncle C. C. is ancient! And you know what he said to me last time he was here? This really hurt my feelings. I had just gotten my guitar and had finally learned 'Blowin' in the Wind' and I came into the living room, trying to be nice, and asked Uncle C. C. if he would like to hear me play. He said, 'Yes, only I hope you're better than whoever's been practicing in the back room.' Mom, *I* had been practicing in the back room!"

"Uncle C. C. is *family*."

Jimmie took this moment to enter the conversation. "But Mom, listen, the car isn't licensed anymore."

"Is that true?" Cassie broke off her objections to Uncle C. C. Her eyes gleamed with excitement. She loved it when her mother did slightly illegal things. "And the car's not even licensed," she would tell her friends. "And it's not a plain car that you wouldn't notice. It's a 1954 DeSoto, and she'll get arrested!"

"Yes, it's true, but there simply isn't enough time

to renew the license by Friday." Mrs. Little added as an afterthought, "No time to renew my license either."

"Mom, you don't even have a driver's license anymore?" Jimmie asked. His voice rose with his increased concern.

"Can I go with you?" Cassie asked, leaning forward.

"You have to work."

"Oh, Mom." Cassie had a job at the Thrift Drugstore during the Christmas rush. "I can get off."

"No, Jimmie will go with me."

Jimmie sat up straighter in his chair. He did not want to be drawn into another unpleasant, danger-filled situation. "Why do I have to go?"

"There may be trouble on the road."

"*May* be!" Cassie said, rolling her eyes comically at Jimmie.

Mrs. Little ignored her. "After supper we'll go down, uncover the car, and see if it will start."

"Let's do it now. I'm not eating this Alpo." Cassie shoved her plate away and the little round pieces of meat rolled around like marbles. She stood up. "After we see about the car, I'll fix us some French fries. Come on."

They went down into the basement, with Mrs. Little leading the way to the car. When she un-

35

covered the DeSoto, she did it reverently. She used elaborate motions. She folded back the covers one by one, moving around the car as if she was on the stage.

"There," she said. She stepped back, then forward to polish an imaginary smear from the front fender. "There," she said again. They could see themselves reflected in the finish.

"Mom, *let* me drive it over to Roger's," Cassie begged.

"No, Cassie."

"I won't even slow down. I'll just drive by and honk. *Please,* Mom."

"Cassie, you can't drive."

"Well, you can't either."

"I can!"

"You can't pass."

"I pass cars all the time."

"You told me it made you so nervous to pass that you had to close your eyes." Cassie opened the door and slipped into the driver's seat. "I'll see if it'll start."

At the front fender, Mrs. Little said, "It'll start." She attributed this to the fact that not one single thing about the car had ever been replaced. The DeSoto even had its original tires, its original seat covers.

36

Cassie turned the key and pressed the gas pedal.

"Make sure it's in neutral," Mrs. Little called, moving out of the way. She had once started the car in first gear, and the car had leaped halfway across the basement.

"It's in neutral. I tell you I know how to drive." As the sound of the engine filled the basement she smiled. She adjusted the rearview mirror. "Now, open the garage door so I can back out."

"No, Cassie." Mrs. Little broke off to say, "Is that the telephone?"

"Want me to get it, Mom?" Jimmie asked.

"No, it'll be Helena." As she started for the stairs, she began twisting her ring on her finger.

"Now open the garage door," Cassie said. "Quick, before Mom gets back." With the eagerness of a three-year-old, she pretended to steer the car.

Jimmie hesitated.

"Come on. Open the door!"

Jimmie walked backward a few steps and then turned. The garage door was opened so seldom that it was hard to lift.

"Hurry!" Cassie cried, impatiently gunning the motor.

The garage door made a loud grating sound as it went up. Jimmie moved to the side and stood by the garbage cans.

"I'm off!" Cassie waved good-bye out the window. "If Mom comes down, tell her I'll be right back. I'll floor it the whole way."

He watched as she drove up the drive. She paused at the street and then turned right. Suddenly Jimmie felt a coldness that had to do with more than the air. He'd done another carelessly stupid thing in opening the garage door. His sister could have an accident and it would be, again, his fault. He could not bear his mother to look at him with those hard, accusing eyes and ask, "Why didn't you stop her?"

He moved back into the garage, fear washing over him. He looked at his watch. It was six-ten.

He paced back and forth on the hard concrete floor of the basement. He paused as he heard a car on the street. He waited. The car drove on down the hill.

"Mom!" he called.

"I'm still on the phone, Jimmie."

He walked from the foot of the stairs to the garbage cans, then back to the stairs. He listened alternately for the DeSoto and his mother.

He looked at his watch. Six-fifteen. Where was Cassie? Roger lived only two blocks away. She should be back by now.

Suddenly he heard a distant siren. He ran quickly up to the street. No car was in sight. The sound of the siren grew fainter. He ran back to the garage, over to the steps. He could hear his mother's voice.

He wrung his hands in an old movie gesture and didn't even know he had done it. It was scary to think that he could be responsible for things he didn't mean to do.

Just when he thought he could bear it no longer—at six-eighteen—Cassie drove down the driveway. The DeSoto, still in first gear, roared into the garage and came to a screeching halt. Cassie bent over the steering wheel, weak with laughter.

"What happened?" he asked anxiously. He was weak, too, wound down from swirling in another whirlpool of fear.

"I got caught on a bush." Cassie doubled over, her neck stretched forward, her shoulders shaking.

"On a what?"

"I was going past Roger's and I wanted to make sure he saw me—that was the whole point, you know—so I was leaning forward to see if he was looking out the window and I went up on the curb and hit a bush."

"Cassie!"

"It's the only bush on the whole block. One bush, and I hit it."

"Cassie, I was really worried."

Cassie laughed again. "I couldn't go forward and

39

I couldn't go backward because this stupid bush was under the bumper. So finally Roger came out and he had these tremendous clippers."

She laughed harder, then stopped as she saw her mother coming down the stairs. "I'll tell you the rest later," she said. Then she raised her voice. "Mom, you don't have a thing to worry about. The car works perfectly."

six

In the front seat of the DeSoto Jimmie and his mother sat upright, bodies as tense as if they were pioneers heading west.

Mrs. Little backed out of the garage and changed gears, and the car lunged forward and stopped. It was these sudden lunges that Mrs. Little could not understand. "What is it *doing*?" she would ask, lifting her hands from the steering wheel to show it was not her fault.

Now, without speaking, she started the car again and steered them out of the driveway. The car swerved onto the street, into the right lane and then into the left where it belonged.

"There," she said when they were safely on their way.

"Can I turn on the radio now?" Jimmie asked. His mother never allowed the radio on while she was experiencing difficulties. He reached for the dial. He loved the dashboard of the car. It gave him the feeling he lived in another time. And when he turned the dial he actually expected to hear music from the fifties. It was a shock when the theme from *Star Wars* filled the car.

"Turn that down," Mrs. Little snapped. There was danger ahead—a four-way stop sign—and she didn't want to be distracted. She gripped the steering wheel tightly.

As they approached the corner she attempted to put on the brakes, but her foot slipped from the brakes and hit the gas pedal, causing them to pick up speed. They raced through the intersection at forty-five miles per hour.

"The car's gone mad!" she cried.

"Take your foot off the gas!"

"It's on the brakes!"

"No, the gas, the gas!"

Taking no chances, she lifted both feet into the air, and the car slowed.

"Now, put on brakes."

Carefully Mrs. Little applied the brakes, and the car came to a complete stop in the middle of the road. Mrs. Little took her hands from the steering wheel to cover her heart. She was breathing fast.

"Are you all right, Mom?"

She nodded.

"You want me to drive?"

She shook her head.

Jimmie never thought of his mother as being old except when he saw her behind the wheel of the DeSoto. Now she stretched forward to take the wheel again. Her right foot reached for the gas pedal.

Slowly, cautiously, she pressed it, and the car moved forward. "Is there anyone behind me?" she asked.

Jimmie glanced over his shoulder. "No."

She sighed with relief at having the road to herself. "It always takes me a while to get used to the car."

Jimmie nodded.

"Once I get out in the country where the roads are straight, I'll be all right."

Jimmie was looking forward to that himself. "Have you ever been stopped by the police?" he asked as she steered them around a corner, using the entire road to complete the turn.

"Yes, but I've never gotten a ticket. They'd just say, 'Try to drive a little more carefully, ma'am.' " She was good at imitating people. "But then I always drive carefully!" She glanced at Jimmie and then quickly back at the road. "I never go over twenty-five unless my foot slips."

"But Mom, driving *slowly* isn't always driving *carefully*. I mean, when you were turning that corner back there, you were driving very slowly, but you were in the wrong lane!" He let his words trail off. It was useless to explain some things to his mother.

She was smiling at herself, "A policeman in Georgia said to me, 'Ma'am, a car is like a loaded gun.'" She gave the policeman a heavy southern accent. "'And when you get in the driver's seat, your hand is on the trigger.' He said that because I was backing into a parking place and went up on the curb and almost hit a meter maid."

She broke off to give her full attention to shifting gears. When she was sure the car was in third gear, she continued. "Then in Tennessee one time, this highway patrolman stopped me and . . ."

She began to imitate, one by one, the policemen who had stopped her, giving the impression that a large part of her life had been spent parked by the side of the road listening to lectures on driving.

Still, Jimmie was grateful she was rambling on. He did not want her to start thinking or talking about Uncle Pete. Although she no longer wept when his name was mentioned, Jimmie felt uneasy when she spoke of him. He understood Conrad, who had asked anxiously, "Did your mom say anything about me?"

"No."

"Did you tell her I was the one who came and got you to watch Uncle Pete?"

"No."

"Whew." In his younger days Conrad had been considered a bad influence by some of the mothers. He was aware of this, and he felt it could certainly be true of Mrs. Little since the accident. "If she does say something, let me know."

Suddenly Jimmie leaned forward in the car. "This is it, Mom." He said it just in time for Mrs. Little to steer into the parking lot of the nursing home and coast to a stop.

"I hope Uncle C. C. is ready," she said, getting out of the car. Now that the tension of driving was over, she sailed across the parking lot.

Inside the nursing home Uncle C. C. was ready, neatly buttoned into his best shirt and suit, but his face was pulled into an unwilling frown.

"Now, why don't you want to go?" the nurse was saying as she adjusted his tie. "You'll have a good time and see all your relatives."

"Uncle C. C.!" Mrs. Little entered the room in a rush. She embraced Uncle C. C. and pulled back to admire him. "You look wonderful."

"I am one hundred years old," he said.

"Now, Mr. Cushman, you're only ninety-two, remember?" the nurse reminded him.

Uncle C. C.'s scowl deepened. "I am one hundred."

Uncle C. C. had learned there were more advantages to being a hundred than any other age. When the Baptist ladies came visiting, they made a special fuss over him because he was a hundred. On Sundays he sometimes stood at the front door and told every visitor, "I am one hundred." Sometimes he thought to add, "today," and was showered with congratulations and candy bars. He intended to be a hundred years old for the rest of his life.

"You be a hundred if you want to," Mrs. Little said soothingly. She patted his jacket lapels. Then she turned and pulled Jimmie forward. "You remember Jimmie, don't you, Uncle Cees?"

Uncle C. C. peered down at Jimmie with his bright eyes. "I never saw him before in my life."

"Now, that just proves my point," Mrs. Little said. "We don't see enough of each other. We are becoming strangers!" She turned to the nurse. "The car's in the parking lot. I left it right out in the middle so Uncle C. C. wouldn't have any trouble getting in."

On the way home the car was quiet. Mrs. Little was concentrating on her driving. Jimmie had nothing to say. Uncle C. C. was silent because something was bothering him. There was something he didn't understand. Something was wrong.

He twisted around to look at Jimmie in the backseat. His small powerful eyes searched for something familiar in Jimmie's face. Then he turned to look at Mrs. Little.

Mrs. Little was at that moment muttering, "Keep going! Keep going!" to a bread truck ahead of her. The bread truck was stopping, and Mrs. Little had never liked to stop on a hill.

"Keep going!" she urged the bread truck. She tried to sound the horn, but was unable to find it. She began to feel around for the hand brake.

Suddenly it occurred to Uncle C. C. what was wrong. "Who is it usually comes to get me?" he asked.

Mrs. Little was too distracted to answer him. "Why would anybody in their right mind stop on a hill?" she asked.

"He's making a delivery, Mom."

"On a *hill*?"

Uncle C. C. said, "A *man* usually comes to get me. He clowns with the nurses."

"Look, now I'm stalled! Are you satisfied?" she yelled at the parked bread truck.

"I *liked* that man." Uncle C. C. glanced with discontent at his present company. Neither the silent boy in the backseat nor the woman beside him yelling at a bread truck was satisfactory company.

"His name was Pete!" Uncle C. C.'s voice rose. His hands began to flutter in his lap. "Where's Pete? Why didn't Pete come for me?"

"Please be quiet until I can get the car started," Mrs. Little said in a low voice.

"But I liked Pete," Uncle C. C. went on. "We always stopped for a beer. Why didn't Pete come for me. Where's Pete?"

"Be quiet!" Mrs. Little snapped.

Uncle C. C. searched for an insult to throw at her. He remembered an old woman at the nursing home who yelled, "Ungrateful trash!" at everyone from her daughter to the head nurse. It seemed especially fitting to Uncle C. C. now. He had come willingly with this woman, freely giving her the pleasure of his company, and now—with insults—this was how she showed her appreciation.

"Ungrateful trash!" he yelled at her.

Mrs. Little did not reply. The only sound in the car was the deep angry breathing of Uncle C. C.

Mrs. Little got the car started on the third try, closed her eyes as she passed the bread truck and drove the rest of the way without speaking.

seven

In the living room Uncle C. C. was telling Cassie a long story about his experiences in the Spanish-American War. Cassie was pretending to pay attention, but she was really listening to her transistor radio.

Uncle C. C. didn't notice. He loved to talk. Actually he had not been in the Spanish-American War at all. He was telling his brother's story. But Uncle C. C. believed you could not hurt a good story by taking the leading role for yourself.

"And so there we were, almost out of ammunition, and a man came along and—"

He glanced up irritably as Mrs. Little entered. Ever since she had yelled, first at the bread truck and then at him, he had not liked her. In his opinion, neither he nor the bread truck had done anything wrong.

"Did you see our Christmas tree, Uncle C. C.?" Mrs. Little asked with false cheerfulness.

He refused to notice it. "At the home," he said, "we have *real* ornaments on our tree."

"Ours are homemade. Cassie did the little dough people and Jimmie—"

"And no lights because they don't want us to burn up." He hoped this would be the end of the Christmas tree conversation. He sometimes wondered how other people could be so boring. He had never once, not in all his years, bored himself.

In a lowered voice Mrs. Little said, "Cassie, have you seen Jimmie?"

"He went out."

"With Conrad?"

"No, by himself."

"Did he go to get the coffee—no, I see the money's still on the counter." She kept her voice low. "I'm worried about Jimmie."

"Why?"

"Well, I think maybe he feels sort of—oh, sort of guilty about Uncle Pete's death."

"Why would he feel guilty?"

"Well, maybe I made him feel that way. I didn't mean to, but you know how I am—I say things without thinking when I'm upset."

50

"Mom, it wasn't his fault at all."

"I know that."

"I mean, let's face it, Uncle Pete was not the usual, normal, everyday uncle."

"Cassie, I don't want to hear that."

"Well, you have to. Uncle Pete's falling through the ice was his own fault and nobody else's. When you take foolish chances with your life, then it's your own fault if you die."

Uncle C. C. was looking from Mrs. Little to Cassie, growing increasingly irritated. He wanted to get back to his story. "Do you want to hear about the war or not?" he asked Cassie impatiently.

Mrs. Little sighed and wiped her hands on her apron. "Go ahead, Uncle Cees," she said. "I've got to get back to the kitchen anyway."

As Mrs. Little left the room, Uncle C. C. turned back to Cassie. "Where was I?" he asked. He was distracted. He considered it inexcusable to interrupt a good story. It was like interrupting the Pope.

"You were almost out of ammo."

"Maybe I better start over."

"No," Cassie said quickly, "I remember the first part. Take it from when you were almost out of ammo."

Down at the river Jimmie was staring at the ice. He was standing a hundred yards downstream from the bridge at an old boat dock. He was alone.

The night before he had had a dream about Uncle Pete. In the dream Uncle Pete's body had been trapped at this very spot. Every detail of the dream had been painfully real, and all morning while he was driving with his mother to the nursing home to get Uncle C. C., he had wanted to be here.

As soon as the DeSoto had come to its shuddering halt in the garage, he had set out. He had run all the way. He had slipped down the bank and skidded onto the ice. Then he had stopped and looked down.

In his dream, the ice at this particular spot had been clear as glass. In his dream Uncle Pete had been right here, face down, his scarf waving in the pale water beneath the ice.

The dream had been so real that Jimmie was surprised to see that the ice here was as thick and green and solid as it was everywhere. He kept staring at the ice.

"Hey, Jimbo!"

Conrad scrambled down the bank; the paper bag he was carrying swung wildly with each step. He looked down at the ice curiously. "You lose something?"

"No, I had this dream about Uncle Pete."

"Oh." Conrad liked to tell his own dreams but not to listen to other people's. "I did my Christmas

52

shopping." He tossed the bag into the air and caught it. Some of the pleasure of Christmas shopping had been lost when Conrad, before leaving the house, had peeped into a few of his own packages. His face fell, remembering. "I'm giving everybody something real nice," he told Jimmie now, "but I'm not getting anything I want. Games, underwear, stuff like that." He shook his head in disgust. "You know, when I was little, I used to get *tons* of toys. My parents would buy out the store!" His voice fell. "Then, as soon as I stopped believing in Santa Claus, they got stingy." His voice rose again. "Which doesn't make sense! I mean, now that I knew it was *them*, it looks like they'd really go all out. Only now I get miserly little gifts—games and underwear. My sister's giving me a T-shirt that says 'Beware of Idiot.' "

"I think I'm getting an encyclopedia."

Conrad gave a moan of sympathy. "I still sort of hope I'm going to get the CB radio, but I sure can't find it." Conrad broke off to say, "Hey, I thought the big family Christmas party was today."

"No, that's tomorrow night."

"Oh." Conrad put his bag of gifts under his arm. "You want to stick around here or are you ready to go?"

"Let's go."

Together they climbed up the bank. "You know

what somebody told me one time about the river?"

"No."

"I think it was my history teacher, Mr. Summers. Anyway he said it was supposed to be called the Monoday River, after somebody named Monoday, but the man who was recording it at the courthouse spelled it Monday. Mr. Summers said there's another river near Elkins called the Tuesday River because people didn't know about the mistake and thought that was the way to name rivers."

He glanced at Jimmie to see if he was interested, but Jimmie was walking along with no expression on his face at all.

Conrad sighed. He liked to see reactions to his stories. He liked laughter, exclamations, burning interest. He secretly felt he was completely capable of going on *The Tonight Show* and becoming a celebrity through his stories. Being with Jimmie, he thought, was like being with a robot. He might as well have been back in his own room, alone, telling himself a story in the mirror. At least then, he thought, he would see some real interest.

Jimmie's thoughts were on his uncle. It would have helped him, he thought, if he *had* found Uncle Pete's body there beneath the ice as he had dreamed. At any rate it would have changed his emotions. He felt now that any change would be for the better.

54

eight

"Hey, did I tell you I was planning a movie?" Conrad asked. They were now passing the bridge. Conrad had been trying to think of something to say all the way up the hill, and this—a genuinely funny, sure-fire amusement—brightened him.

Jimmie shook his head.

"Science fiction—*comedy* science fiction," Conrad said. "It's about this space person—" He began to laugh in anticipation of what was coming. "This'll break you up," he predicted. "And this space person's been watching TV, see, so he'll know how to look and act when he gets to earth. He's going to pass himself off as an earth person. So he knows, see, from TV ads, that he's got to smell good or he won't have any friends. Only up there on his planet bad smells are considered *good*, and *good* smells *bad*. So!" Conrad's face was red with enthusiasm. He started laughing again at the possibilities of his story.

"*So!* He makes this stuff and sprays it under his arms, on his hair, everywhere. The odor, Jimbo, is a cross between rotten eggs and horse manure, and now he's ready to come to earth."

He glanced over at Jimmie, expecting to see Jimmie laughing, at least smiling. Instead, Jimmie was walking along in the same blank way. There was still no expression on his face.

Conrad stopped. He was both hurt and angry. He felt he had suffered enough from Jimmie's lack of interest. He said, "Look, would you mind telling me just how long you're going to keep this up?"

"What do you mean?" Jimmie stumbled as he looked up. He was puzzled.

"I mean that everybody else has gotten back to their normal selves but you. Even your mom's all right now. She's throwing a party."

Jimmie was startled. He had been so wrapped in his own unhappiness that he had not even been aware of Conrad. He tried to think of something to say.

"I mean, why don't you just snap out of it!" Conrad surprised himself by using one of his mother's phrases and, indeed, his mother's voice as he spoke.

56

His face, brows drawn together in anger, felt like his mother's face too.

They were now at the very spot where Uncle Pete had begun his walk on the Monday River, but neither boy noticed.

Jimmie said flatly, "You don't understand."

"I do understand. Bad things have happened to me too, you know."

"What?"

Conrad struggled with his memory. He did a mental pan of his life. He could not find one event terrible enough to fit this occasion.

"Has *your* father ever gotten killed in a coal mine?" Jimmie asked, breaking the silence in a cold emotionless voice. "Has *your* uncle ever drowned in the Monday River while you were standing there watching?"

He broke off. He felt himself slipping into one of those terrible contests where you claim your own life, your own pain, is worse than anybody else's. In this case it was true, but Conrad was an unworthy opponent.

He suddenly saw Conrad as one of those unfeeling, uncaring people who never let anything bother them. People who go through life playing that game of hot potato. As soon as they feel anything unpleasant—any guilt, any unhappiness—they toss to somebody else.

Jimmie was absolutely certain that Conrad would not understand what he was feeling in a million years. "You don't understand," he said again, flatly, finally.

Conrad was always deeply hurt when someone told him he did not understand. It was an insult. His voice, his manner turned cold.

"I understand that I don't want to be around you anymore," Conrad said.

"You think *I* want to be around *you*?" Jimmie asked. His eyebrows rose in astonishment.

"I mean *ever*," Conrad yelled. His face was thrust forward. His mouth remained open as if the word "ever" was still coming out.

They stared at each other. Out of the past two days of confusion and conflict, only one thing was clear to Jimmie. He no longer liked Conrad. He also was aware that Conrad no longer liked him.

Jimmie turned quickly and started up the hill alone. His face was flushed with anger.

Conrad followed. He was dissatisfied with the argument, discontented with himself. He felt that he had not gotten his full say, that he had not hurt Jimmie in the way Jimmie had hurt him.

He moved closer behind Jimmie. Jimmie could hear him. Conrad was swinging his bag of Christmas gifts at Jimmie's back. He stepped forward in a sort of tribal dance step, barely missing Jimmie with each swing.

This was the kind of thing that infuriated Jimmie. He was so angry now that he felt he was going to cry. He whirled.

"You touch me with that bag," he warned, "just *touch* me with it, and you'll be sorry."

Conrad's eyes were wide with innocence, but his mouth smirked. He swung the bag so that it brushed the air in front of Jimmie's chest. Jimmie did not move. He waited, hating the look on Conrad's face.

Conrad swung the bag again. It came closer this time, but still did not touch Jimmie. Conrad's smile widened.

Suddenly Jimmie lashed out and tore the bag from Conrad's hands. It fell to the ground with a crash. Notepaper spilled onto the pavement and fluttered in the wind. Gardenia cologne ran down the sidewalk. The scent, sickeningly sweet, rose between Jimmie and Conrad.

Without a word of warning, Conrad hit Jimmie on the chin. It was a perfectly thrown, perfectly timed punch. It was a punch so solid nothing more was needed. Jimmie fell backward onto the sidewalk.

The smell of gardenia cologne choked him. Tears

of rage ran down his cheeks. He felt as if every bad emotion in the world was raging inside him. Guilt, hatred, anger, fear, unhappiness—all struggled for supremacy.

Conrad rubbed his hand. He looked with deep satisfaction on Jimmie's sprawled body. Mentally he began to count to ten. Mentally he awarded himself a knockout.

Without a word he bent to retrieve his ruined gifts. The spilled cologne strengthened his self-righteous feeling. He made a point of elaborately discarding the broken cologne bottle. Then he got up and walked away.

After a moment Jimmie got to his feet. With his eyes down, he walked to his house and opened the kitchen door.

In the living room Uncle C. C. had at last finished the story of the Spanish-American War. He looked as contented as if he'd eaten a ten-course meal.

Cassie asked, "But didn't it make you feel bad?"

"What?"

"Killing all those people."

Instantly Uncle C. C. sat erect. He began to tremble with indignation. He vibrated like an old appliance.

"I have never killed anyone in my life!"

"But—"

"I value life!"

"But Uncle Cees, you just said that in the war you and your company killed I don't know how many men."

"Oh."

Uncle C. C. swallowed. He leaned back in his chair. His arms were still trembling. His hands fluttered like moths over his knees.

"Didn't it make you feel bad?" Cassie asked again. She appeared interested in him for the first time.

Since it was actually his brother's story, his brother's war, Uncle C. C. had no idea. That was the only trouble with adopting other people's stories, he thought. You didn't have all the details. He let all the air out of his old lungs.

In the kitchen Jimmie leaned against the door and waited for Uncle C. C.'s answer. His face throbbed with pain. He wiped his tears on his jacket sleeve.

"No," Uncle C. C. said firmly. "It didn't make me feel bad. They were the enemy."

When Jimmie heard that, he knew that he and Uncle C. C. were separated by more than age. They could have been born in different worlds instead of just different centuries. Jimmie imagined Uncle C. C. had been raised in a simple time when good boys became president and bad boys became crooks, and the enemy wasn't a real, flesh-and-blood person at all. Now, in his own complicated age, good and bad ran together like dye and nothing was simple.

"Jimmie," his mother called from her room, "did you remember to get the coffee?"

"No."

"I'm going to need it for the party."

Silence.

"So would you go get it now before the store closes?"

"Yes."

"The money's on the counter."

He took the five-dollar bill from the counter and went back out the door. His face was without expression. His eyes were on the ground.

The only sign that a tornado of rage and hatred was swirling inside him was that in his pocket, he was kneading the five-dollar bill into a small hard ball.

nine

"Too bad about your uncle."

"Yes." Jimmie nodded his head without turning around. He was standing in the express checkout lane at Kroger's. He had a can of coffee in his hand.

"How's your mom taking it?"

"Fine."

He still did not look back at Mr. Hunter, nor did he mention that his mother was at this moment happily preparing for a party. That was hard even for him to understand.

Ahead a woman shopper took her bag of groceries and left. Jimmie moved forward two more steps. He shifted the can of coffee to his other hand.

"I don't guess they found the body."

"No."

It was his turn at last. He set the can of coffee on the counter and began to unfold his five-dollar bill. The checkout girl waited with a look of bored fatigue on her face. He spread the bill on the counter, ironing it flat with his hands.

"Another man tried to walk across the river a couple of years ago—one of the Sidler brothers."

Jimmie turned quickly, interested at last. "Did he make it?"

"No, he turned back when the ice started creaking."

"Oh."

"That's what your uncle should have done."

Again Jimmie nodded. He left the store holding the coffee in both hands. Slowly he started for home.

The wind was blowing up from the river now, and a few snowflakes swirled around the streetlights. He noticed none of this, just walked with his eyes down.

When he opened the kitchen door, Cassie was at the sink, peeling potatoes. She whirled around. "Don't go in the living room," she hissed, "or you'll have to listen to Uncle C. C. tell about—" She broke off. "What happened to your face?" she asked.

Jimmie ran his tongue over his lip. He realized now it was swollen. "Nothing."

"Let me see."

"It's nothing." He jerked his arm away from her,

set the coffee on the table and started for his room. She caught up with him in the hall. She was drying her hands on her shirt.

"Did somebody hit you?"

"No."

"Who was it? Conrad?"

"Nobody hit me."

He went into his room and pulled the door shut behind him. Cassie opened it at once and came in.

"What's wrong."

He turned his head away. He shook his head to stop her questions.

When Cassie wanted to, Jimmie thought, she could be as kind and gentle as a madonna, more so even than his mother. He didn't think he could bear kindness now.

"Leave me alone," he said. He sat down on the bed, his face turned to the window.

Cassie sat down beside him. Jimmie felt the springs give with her weight.

"Are you worried about what Mother said?" she asked in a voice so soft, so kind, he wanted to cry.

"No."

"Because you're not to blame for Uncle Pete's death."

"I know that."

"I'm not sure you do. Look, Jimmie, things like

this—feeling guilty about something you couldn't help—well, it can mess up your whole life."

"I don't feel guilty exactly." He looked down at his feet. "I just feel, well—" He paused. He thought the hardest question anybody ever had to answer was Did I do enough? It was like trying to see both sides of yourself, front and back, at the same time.

"I just feel," he started again, "well, that if I could do it over again, well, I would try harder. No, I would stop him. I don't care what I would have had to do. I would stop him."

"I know you would." She folded her hands in her lap and looked at him.

"It's hard to put into words," he said.

"I felt sort of the same way after Dad died."

He looked at her. "But why? He died in the mine. It didn't have anything to do with you."

"The night before he died—you won't remember this—but the night before he died we had an argument, a really awful, senseless argument."

"What about?"

"I wanted a pair of twenty-five-dollar loafers and he wouldn't let me get them."

"You and Dad used to argue about stuff like that all the time. You seemed to enjoy it."

"Yes, but this time I said, 'You don't care anything about me,' and stamped out of the room. And that was the last thing I ever said to him."

He watched her without speaking.

"It took me a long, long time to get over saying that. It still bothers me sometimes."

Cassie's blue eyes brimmed with tears. Jimmie glanced away, out the window at the cold, gray afternoon. It was, he thought, the perfect setting for what was happening in his house—not one spot of brightness or sunlight or warmth.

"So I know how something you can never take back can make you feel." She reached out and hugged him. "You are not alone."

She got to her feet quickly and left the room.

In the hall she collided with Uncle C. C. "There you are!" he cried. "I was looking for you. Want to hear about the time I got arrested in Oklahoma City?"

ten

Jimmie lay in his bed, looking at the ceiling. Despite Cassie's conversation, her understanding, he still felt isolated. He imagined the entire rest of the world at this moment to be singing carols of joy, an enormous choir in a cathedral. He alone stood outside . . . in the snow . . . bareheaded. . . .

"People die when they're ready to die," Uncle C. C. announced abruptly, breaking off Jimmie's thoughts.

Jimmie raised up on one elbow and looked at Uncle C. C., who was in the twin bed across the room.

Uncle C. C. had been on the subject of death off and on ever since they had gone to bed. This was because just before bedtime Mrs. Little had finally

gotten around to telling Uncle C. C. the story of
Uncle Pete's accident.

"Yes, people die when they're ready to die," he
repeated. He spoke with conviction because he believed this with all his heart.

Jimmie digested the thought. He found it warmed
and chilled him at the same time, chilled him because it suggested that Uncle Pete had been ready
for that thin patch of ice. It warmed him because it
meant that he—who was not at all ready for death—
would not die until he was.

"There's two parts to a man's life," Uncle C. C.
went on. He glanced over at Jimmie with his small
sharp eyes. "Forget all the junk you've heard about
youth, teenage, middle age, old age."

Jimmie nodded.

"There's two parts to a man's life—up and down."
Uncle C. C. was particularly fond of this idea because he felt he himself was still on the way up.

"Your life goes up like a fly ball." He lifted his
arm to show the path. "And then, like it or not, it
starts down. And when it starts down, *you know it*.
It's like going over the top of a roller coaster."
Uncle C. C. was sure of the sensation even though
he himself had never been on a roller coaster. "Your
stomach lurches, and when that happens, when you
start down, that's *it*." His hand, in a deep dive, fell

69

to the covers.

Again Jimmie nodded.

"The people who are lucky have a long, long up and a quick down."

In his bed, Uncle C. C. had a pleased expression on his face. He liked to talk about death. Indeed, he enjoyed imagining his own death. He saw it as an epic struggle. After all, as a unique human being, he owed it to the world to struggle. When he was gone, the world would never find anybody to take his place.

"Let me tell you what my death's going to be like."

"All right."

"It's going to be like a picture I saw in a Bible book when I was little. It was called 'Jacob Wrestling with the Angel of God.' And the angel was enormous, with great big wings that beat the air, and a light that shone like the sun, and Jacob was kicking and struggling for his life."

He rested against his pillow. "That's the way it will be with me." As he lay there he could feel the wings against him, see the lights, feel himself finally relaxing as the enormous angel bore him skyward. "I don't believe in giving up," he said.

"Well, no," Jimmie said. "Me either."

"There's an old woman at the home who whines all the time. 'I want to die,' she says." He whined like the old woman and then became himself again. "I stick my face right up to hers and yell, 'Go ahead!' " He settled his covers more firmly over his chest. "You know what she said to me one time?"

"What?"

"She said, 'Life has no meaning.' " Uncle C. C. became agitated just remembering it. "Meaning!" he repeated. He was sputtering with anger now, trembling. People today had too much. That was their trouble. They sat in the middle of life like babies in a room full of toys and whined to be amused. His voice rose because he was now on his very favorite subject.

"She demanded *meaning* when life is a *miracle*! Air to breathe, hundreds of vegetables, thousands of fruits, trees that turn green in the spring and red in the fall." His voice, high with excitement, made miracles of the things he mentioned. "Alaska *and* Florida. A sun *and* a moon. Oceans *and* deserts. Summer *and* winter."

He paused. He drew in a deep breath to calm himself. "And giraffes," he said finally.

"Giraffes?"

Uncle C. C. nodded. He had always had a fondness for the giraffe. He considered the giraffe a special comic miracle. It was as if God had said, "Look what I can throw in for good measure."

"And bears as white as the snow," he went on, "and horses black as night, and then little tiny horses that swim in the sea." He considered the sea horse another comic miracle. "And this stupid, whining woman couldn't see *the meaning*." His voice rose to imitate the old woman's whine.

His hands began to make restless movements on the covers. He could see the woman clearly in his mind now. She had cringed back from his fury, genuinely afraid. She had held up her thin arms for protection. This had only made him madder. He had wished for his grandfather's cane with its huge silver knob so he could bop her over the head. "You want meaning," he had screeched, "look at a giraffe."

"Don't get upset," Jimmie said, alarmed by the red splotches that were appearing on Uncle C. C.'s face and neck.

"I'm not, I'm not."

Uncle C. C. began to take deep breaths to calm himself. He recalled that at the home, it had taken three nurses to stop the argument—one to rescue the old woman and two to put him to bed with a sedative.

In the bedroom across the hall Cassie suddenly cried, "Mom, what happened to my goldfish?"

"What do you mean?"

"One of them's dead. Look! And Mom, these are Roger's Christmas present." Her voice rose with her distress. "What am I going to *do*? I already told him I was giving him *two* goldfish."

"Don't bother me with that now, Cassie," Mrs. Little said. She was trying to remember if she had invited every single relative. "Did I call Aunt Catherine?"

"I told that woman I wanted healthy goldfish!" Cassie said through tight lips. She stormed into the bathroom, holding the dead goldfish by the tail.

There was the sound of the toilet being flushed.

"And tomorrow the stores are closed!" she said as she came out of the bathroom.

Jimmie was still raised up on one elbow, watching Uncle C. C. Uncle C. C.'s profile was all sharp angles, the nose of an old Indian, the chin of a witch. His long pale hands were folded over his chest.

When Jimmie had first learned that Uncle C. C. was going to share his room, he had been filled with dread. "I'm afraid," he had finally confessed to his mother and Cassie.

"Afraid of Uncle Cees?" Cassie had asked. "You could knock him over with a wet noodle."

"I just don't want him in my room, that's all."

"Well, where else is he going to sleep?" Mrs. Little asked.

"Cassie could sleep with you and he could have her room."

"No. And anyway, he might wake up in the middle of the night and get confused. I want someone with him." There was such finality in Mrs. Little's voice that Jimmie knew it was useless to protest anymore.

Now that it was a fact, now that Uncle C. C. was there in the opposite twin bed, Jimmie realized he was glad to have him. It made him less lonely.

"Uncle Cees?"

Uncle C. C. did not open his eyes. "What?"

"Do you mind if I ask you something?"

"Go ahead."

"Well, I don't see how it's possible to kill somebody, even the enemy, and not feel bad about it."

Uncle C. C.'s eyes snapped open. "Kill people?"

"Yes, in the war."

"Oh, the war."

"Yes, the Spanish-American War."

"Oh." Uncle C. C.'s face was suddenly twisted with indecision. He loved the Spanish-American War story. He had told it so often it was his, the way a certain role actually belongs to the actor who performs it successfully. He sighed with deep regret.

"If you must know," he said in a low voice, "I didn't kill anybody."

"Even in the war?"

"I wasn't in the war," Uncle C. C. said with what he thought was great patience.

"But you told Cassie—"

"I *know* what I told Cassie!" Now his patience was gone, worn thin by what he considered repeated stupidity. His fire returned. "I was just making a *story* out of it. I was *entertaining*."

"Oh."

There was a silence while Uncle C. C. regained his composure. "The truth is," he went on, "I never killed anybody in my life. I value life."

"I do too."

"I went hunting *one time*, shot a rabbit. It was by accident more than anything."

"Oh?"

"And when I looked at that dead rabbit, I said to myself, 'I'm not ever going to do this again.' "

Jimmie continued to watch Uncle C. C. He was waiting. But Uncle C. C.'s eyes closed. Finally Jimmie said, "But what if you had killed something without meaning to? What if—"

Uncle C. C.'s face was relaxed now. A faint sound, too weak to be a snore, came from his open mouth.

"Good night, Uncle Cees," Jimmie said. He lay back against his pillow.

In the living room Mrs. Little began quietly playing 'Silent Night.'

Jimmie closed his eyes and slept.

eleven

"Mom, now the *other* goldfish is dead!"

Cassie's voice awakened Jimmie. It was morning. The pale winter sun shone through the one window of Jimmie's bedroom and lit up Uncle C. C.'s bed. Jimmie lay without moving, eyes closed, and waited.

"Mom!"

"I heard you, Cassie."

"So what am I going to give Roger now—this bowl of water?"

"You'll think of something."

"I *won't*."

"All right, then, how about this: Your Aunt Helena has guppies. Call her and ask if—"

"Guppies!" Cassie's voice betrayed her horror. "Mom, guppies are only about that long."

76

"Well, it's better than nothing."

"Mom, you don't understand anything! Roger is giving me a sterling silver bracelet with my initials on it. I can't give him guppies!"

The toilet flushed. The door to Cassie's room slammed shut. Then there was silence.

Jimmie glanced over at Uncle C. C. Uncle C. C.'s eyes were closed, but Jimmie knew the loud yelling in the hall had awakened him.

Uncle C. C. was awake, and his feet were cold. He felt as if he were a boy again, swimming in the pond behind his grandpa's house. The water was always warm on top, but underneath, where the springs were, it was as cold as ice. Uncle C. C. shifted his feet. He became aware that the bed he was in was not his own.

"Where am I?" he asked without opening his eyes.

"You're at our house," Jimmie told him, "Remember, we're having a family party today."

"Oh, yes." He paused. "When do I get to go home?"

"Tomorrow morning."

Uncle C. C. sighed.

"I'm going to need some help," Mrs. Little called cheerfully from the hall. She banged on Jimmie's door, then Cassie's. "Children, I need some help."

They worked all morning getting ready for the

party. Jimmie made the beds. Mrs. Little cooked. Cassie vacuumed. Uncle C. C. made their work lighter by telling them the story of how he became the spelling champion of Monroe County at age ten.

In the back of his mind he knew it was his sister Eunice who had really been in the spelling bee. He knew too that she had lost, been spelled down by a girl named Wilma Darrell on the word "receipt."

In this, the revised edition of the story, he himself took the starring role. It was he who spelled the word correctly, and Wilma Darrell who suffered defeat. There in the Littles' living room, while Cassie pushed the vacuum around him, he spelled the word again. "R-e-c-e-i-p-t."

He had a perfect memory for the old times and could even remember the letter which his sister had omitted and stress it. But he had absolutely no idea who this girl was who was vacuuming around his feet.

"Oh, I'm getting excited," Mrs. Little said.

"I know, Mom."

"I just hope everybody doesn't bring cranberry salad."

The telephone rang and Mrs. Little went to answer it. She returned to the living room, sighing angrily. "That is the fourth time this morning that I have answered the telephone and no one is there.

78

Who could be doing that?"

Jimmie knew instantly that it was Conrad. Conrad considered the telephone the perfect instrument for revenge. It allowed him to bother people without their knowing who it was.

"I've got to take a break," Mrs. Little said. She moved toward the piano.

Jimmie enjoyed it when she played, smoothly, beautifully, her slim hands so firm on the keys she seemed never to make a mistake. He liked it less when her pupils came for lessons, working their way painfully through the John Thompson books, stumbling over "The Spinning Song," crossing their hands awkwardly on "To a Skyscraper."

Now she began to play Christmas songs. "Have you a favorite, Uncle Cees?"

" 'O Holy Night.' "

Without missing a note Mrs. Little slid into the requested song. Cassie began to sing. Jimmie thought it was as if the party had already started.

The phone rang.

"Not again," Mrs. Little said.

"I'll get it." Jimmie went into the kitchen and picked up the phone. "Hello?"

As he expected there was no answer, only the faint sound of breathing.

"Hello," he said again.

Silence.

"I know this is you, Conrad."

Silence.

Jimmie put the phone back on the hook with an angry bang. In the living room his mother swung into "Silent Night."

Jimmie bent over the telephone, his face flushed. He dialed Conrad's number. The phone was answered on the first ring, confirming Jimmie's suspicion that Conrad was sitting by the phone.

"Hello?" Conrad said.

Jimmie did not answer.

"Hello!"

Jimmie waited in a tense, expectant silence.

"I know this is you, Jimmie," Conrad said in a rush. "I can hear your mom playing in the background."

"How do you know it's *my* mom," Jimmie demanded, "unless you just called *me* and heard her?"

The phone clicked in his ear as Conrad hung up. Quickly, fingers shaking, he dialed Conrad's number. He got a busy signal. He dialed again.

"Jimmie, don't play with the telephone," Mrs. Little called from her piano bench.

"I'm not." He had never felt less playful in his life. He dialed again. His anger caused him to misdial, and a strange woman said, "Harker residence."

He hung up the phone. He was trembling. Face

determined, he began to dial Conrad's number again. Then he stopped and put the phone down.

In the living room, spirits were rising. His mother began a jazzed-up version of "Jingle Bells."

"Come on, Jimmie," Cassie called. "We need somebody to sing harmony."

"Not right now."

He went in and sat down on his bed. He concentrated on not feeling anything. He tried to wipe his body absolutely clean of emotions.

What he really wanted, he realized as he sat there, was to get back to the normal, everyday way he had felt Wednesday when he was standing by the clothes drier waiting for his blue jeans. You didn't appreciate normal, everyday life until it was gone.

But that seemed hopeless now, a miracle in an age when miracles, like dinosaurs, had become extinct. The best thing he could do, he thought, was just to keep juggling his terrible feelings—the guilt, the fear, the anger, the hatred, the misery. Because if they all settled upon him at once, he would be crushed.

"Jimmeeeee, we neeeeed you," Cassie called.

He continued to sit on the edge of the bed.

" 'Jingle Bells' neeeeeeds you."

"I'm coming."

He got up and walked slowly into the living room. He arrived just in time to join in the second chorus.

twelve

Since the party had begun, Mrs. Little had gotten younger before Jimmie's eyes. All the relatives had. They had arrived old, and now, one hour into the party, they all had young faces, rosy childlike faces on wrinkled necks and stout bodies.

On the sofa Great-Aunt Hilda was swinging her swollen ankles like an excited girl. She was telling Uncle C. C. about the time Uncle Pete had told fortunes at the church bazaar.

"I believed he was a real gypsy!" she said.

Jimmie was on the sofa too, squashed between Aunt Hilda and Uncle C. C. He felt that he alone had an old, unhappy face.

"And he was wearing *my* wig. He borrowed *my* wig without my knowing it and I *still* didn't recognize him!"

82

She laughed at herself. Uncle C. C., who had not laughed out loud in seventeen years, bobbed his head. Jimmie nodded too. He felt as false as an actor on the stage pretending to enjoy a party.

"That was one of Pete's greatest talents. He could be *anybody*."

Aunt Helena said, "That is so true. One time we were watching the Junior Miss America Pageant and right before our eyes he *became* Miss Wisconsin, buck teeth and all. He sang 'Climb Every Mountain' right along with her, and you couldn't have told the difference. You remember that, Karena?"

"Yes. He could imitate anybody and any language. One time on the bus he started speaking *Chinese!*"

"It's his German I'll always remember."

Across the room Uncle Henry was telling a story of his own about a dog Pete had owned. At the peak of the story he broke into a comical howl. Since he did it well, they all recognized the howl and cried, "Blue Boy!" The sisters laughed.

Great-Aunt Hilda rested one hand on Jimmie's leg. She patted him fondly. "One thing about Pete— while he lived, he was *alive*."

"You want to know about Pete? I'll tell you about Pete!" Uncle C. C. volunteered. Actually he had no story in mind, but he was sure he would have by the time he got into the conversation.

"Excuse me," Jimmie said.

He got up and went into the kitchen. He got a glass of water and sipped it slowly, his eyes on the people in the living room.

The kitchen door burst open. Cousin Libby entered. "Did I miss anything?" she asked. Without waiting for an answer she said, "Here, Jimmie, do something with this salad," and went into the living room. "You can start talking now," she cried, "I'm here."

"Libby!"

The family cried their welcome in unison. They twirled around her, then moved back into groups. It looked to Jimmie like a disorganized square dance.

Abruptly Jimmie put down his glass. He opened the kitchen door and stepped outside.

The evening sky was cloudy and the air was cold. He breathed deeply. The cold air felt good on his face. With his hands in his pockets, he walked slowly down the steps.

He crossed the yard as if he was pacing off a distance. He felt like a participant in a solitary duel. At the oak tree he turned. He looked at the party through the picture window.

He leaned back against the tree. Now that he was outside, separated from the party physically as well as in spirit, he found he could watch the family with a sort of detachment.

In front of the Christmas tree, Mrs. Little was standing with her two sisters, Helena and Karena. They were getting ready to sing. As girls they had had a brief local singing career, and they could still remember the old songs, words and gestures.

"Helena, Karena and Laurena" they had been called, "The Singing Ford Sisters." They had been glad that when their mother had named them, she had thought to add A's to their names for elegance. They thought it would look good when they became famous.

Now, as they began singing, they looked like the girls they had once been. It was easy to imagine them on the stage of the school auditorium, in front of the church, at the radio station.

"More! More!" Cousin Frances cried when they finished.

"No, that's enough of us," Mrs. Little protested, throwing up her hands.

"But I missed the largest part of it. I was in the bathroom!" Cousin Frances was on her feet now, protesting the injustice like a lawyer. Great-Aunt Hilda joined her.

"At least do 'All I Want for Christmas Is My Two Front Teeth.' "

"Oh, we don't know the words to that anymore,"

Mrs. Little said. "Besides, that was Pete's song. We just did the background music."

"I'll take Pete's part," Uncle Henry offered.

"Remember now, he always sang it with a lisp."

"How could I forget?"

Cousin Frances plopped herself down on the rug, arms folded, and waited. Her face, like those of the others, shone with anticipation.

Outside, Jimmie no longer noticed the cold. It was as if he was watching a television show. Looking at his family like this, as if they belonged to someone else, made him see them in a different way. The flurry of activity as they got ready for the song gave him a flash of pleasure.

This was the first good emotion Jimmie had felt in three days. He welcomed it. He felt the pleasure, small as it was, spread over him like a drop of oil on water.

In the picture window, Mrs. Little and her sisters began to sing "All I Want for Christmas Is My Two Front Teeth." Uncle Henry had, somewhat unsuccessfully, attempted to black out two of his teeth with an eyebrow pencil. As he came forward, grinning, everyone burst into laughter.

Jimmie smiled too. He felt he had not smiled in at least a hundred years. He was surprised his face did not crack under the pressure like hardened clay.

Leaning against the tree, he continued to watch his family.

They were the ones, he saw now, who could help him. They were like a cocoon, something to break out of one day when he was ready, but right now he wanted to join them. He wanted to give in to their laughter and fun, to ease his bad feelings by recalling good times. He wanted to have their good feelings dropped, one by one, like antacids, into his body. He hoped that one day, with luck, when he came out of the cocoon, he would see himself as he now saw each of them—as a unique, one-of-a-kind individual who had never been on this earth before and never would be again.

He stepped forward. He felt as if he was moving forward in more ways than just a few physical steps. And then abruptly he stopped. His body tensed. He saw that someone was creeping around the side of the house.

The figure, bent low, passed under the picture window, then straightened. The figure pressed back into the bushes, face turned to the window.

Someone had come to spy on his family's party! Jimmie took one silent step toward him.

thirteen

Slowly, step by step, Jimmie began to move closer to the figure in the bushes. Above him, the wind rustled the remaining dead leaves of the oak tree. A dry stick broke beneath Jimmie's foot.

Sensing something, the person glanced over his shoulder, a quick nervous glance, but he failed to see Jimmie under the branches of the tree.

The figure turned back to the window, but in that instant, in the light from the window, Jimmie had seen who it was. It was Conrad.

"What do you think you're doing?" Jimmie asked in a quiet, accusing voice.

Conrad jerked his head around so quickly that his neck popped. He drew in his breath. "Don't do that to me," he said. He put one hand over his heart.

Jimmie answered his own question. "You are spying on our party."

"You know I don't like people to sneak up on me. You're lucky I didn't have an attack."

"Well, just what are you doing spying on our party? That's what I'd like to know."

"Well, what are you doing out here?" Conrad countered. "You're supposed to be inside."

They looked at each other, a long hard look. Each weighed the other's offense—spying on the party versus deserting the party.

In the picture window behind them Helena was pulling Uncle C. C. to his feet. She began to lead him in a one-sided polka.

"One, two three. One, two three."

"I'm too old," he protested. "I'm ninety-two!" In his agitation he forgot his vow to be a hundred years old for the rest of his life and actually gave his real age.

"Come on, Uncle Cees, you used to polka like a lunatic. Let's show them. Here we go. Right foot first. One, two three. One, two three."

The sudden laughter and cheers as Uncle C. C. yielded to the pressure and did three polka steps caused Conrad to turn back to the window.

"Did you see what happened? What'd I miss?"

Jimmie continued to look at the back of Conrad's

head. He still felt angry with Conrad. He wished he could forgive people the way his mother did. She actually *loved* to forgive people—she had told him so—and she did it beautifully, with her arms outstretched like a madonna.

He forgave, when he forgave at all, reluctantly, stingily, painfully. At one time he had hoped forgiving people was one of those things that would pop out naturally with adulthood, like whiskers, but he had begun to suspect it was not.

"That old man can still dance," Conrad said as he watched Uncle C. C. in the picture window.

Jimmie moved beside Conrad. He could see Conrad's face now. In the light from the window, it shone with admiration.

Jimmie was still struggling with himself. He told himself it was Conrad who owed him an apology. Only he knew Conrad never apologized. Never. Once Conrad had endured a month of detention halls rather than tell Miss Markham he was sorry he had made gestures behind her back.

Conrad's way of forgiving was to start acting normal again. Jimmie knew that was what Conrad was doing now because his voice was his own and not his mother's.

He could do that too—just start acting normal and they would be friends again. Instead he made himself say, "I'm sorry about your Christmas presents."

Conrad turned, genuinely surprised at this unasked-for apology. He gallantly dismissed the Christmas presents with a shrug.

"Did you get some more cologne for your mom?"

"No, I got her powder. That perfume stank."

Jimmie nodded. He felt he would never smell that particular scent again without becoming ill.

"No wonder she never used it before."

"Was your sister's notepaper ruined?"

"I put the dirty sheets on the bottom. It worked out."

Conrad turned back to the window as more laughter came from the house. "You got a crazy family," he said. His face was envious.

"Thank you," Jimmie said. He made a mental comparison between his lively family and Conrad's bland one. He was proud to be part of the colorful group inside. "I've got to go in," he said.

"Do you have to?"

"I want to."

"Oh," Conrad said. He made an unsuccessful effort not to look pitiful. "I'll just stand out here for a few minutes and watch, if you don't mind."

Jimmie hesitated. He recalled how he had felt the other night, mentally standing outside the entire world. "You can come inside, I guess, if you want to."

"Come to the party?"

"Sure." Jimmie felt another good emotion—generosity—as he shared his family. One by one, the old torments were being replaced. Every bad emotion, it seemed, had an opposite.

"What would your mother say?"

"Nothing. Cassie invited Roger, so I guess I can invite an outsider too."

Conrad hesitated. He put his hands in his pockets. "Did you tell your mom I hit you?"

"No."

"Then I'll come."

They walked to the back door and entered the kitchen. In the living room Uncle Henry said, "A toast! A toast!" There was a rustle and scramble for wine glasses.

"We'll drink to the man we're celebrating," Uncle Henry said. "To Pete!"

The whole family, Jimmie included, said, "To Pete!" in beautiful unison. Beside Jimmie, Conrad muttered happily, "To Pete." It was his first toast. He looked around for something to drink.

Jimmie glanced again at his family as they lifted their glasses. At that moment they all had clear sharp outlines, like figures in a coloring book.

"Here," Conrad said.

He handed Jimmie a Pepsi, and they snapped off the tabs and drank with the family.

In the living room the three sisters began singing "Silent Night." As the others joined in, Mrs. Little slipped onto the piano bench and began the accompaniment.

For the first time Jimmie felt the peace they were singing about.

"Nice party," Conrad said.

fourteen

"I *know* Roger was disappointed in his guppies," Cassie said. She was sitting by the Christmas tree in a nest of torn wrapping paper.

"Why?" Mrs. Little asked without glancing up. She was engrossed in a music book she had gotten for Christmas. "Did he say something?"

"No." Cassie kicked the loose paper disgustedly. Christmas trees and smiling Santas fluttered around her feet. "I just feel terrible."

"Why is that?" Mrs. Little still had not looked up. She could carry on an intelligent conversation in her sleep.

"Well, wouldn't you feel terrible if someone gave you a sterling silver bracelet *and* an album and you gave them guppies?"

94

"No, it's the thought that counts."

"Huh! That's easy for you to say. You gave *and* got nice gifts." Cassie eyed the Spanish shawl around her mother's shoulders, a gift from her sisters.

A silence fell over the four people sitting in the living room. Uncle C. C. broke the silence with a loud impatient snort.

He was sitting at the window, staring sullenly out at the rain. He wanted to go back to the nursing home. He had started asking to be driven back at seven o'clock that morning, but Mrs. Little refused to drive in the rain.

"But I don't *mind* going in the rain," Uncle C. C. had said, at first with great patience. He accepted the fact that Mrs. Little, out of consideration for his age, might not want to subject him to bad weather. But as the morning wore on, and she still refused to take him, he grew sullen.

He now stared meanly at the rain. He felt, for the first time in his life, critical of Mother Nature. He believed she was slipping.

As he sat there, he realized that he hadn't seen a breathtaking sunset in years. He couldn't remember when he'd seen a really colorful rainbow. And summer rains weren't as refreshing as those he had run naked through as a boy. And water didn't taste as pure. And snows weren't as soft and clean as those

95

he had rolled in with his brothers.

Yes, Mother Nature was slipping, he thought. And here, just outside the window, was final proof. When she got a rain going, she no longer knew when to stop it.

He shifted impatiently in his chair. He had the uncomfortable feeling that he was missing some important event at the home. Maybe the Baptist ladies with their haystack hairdos were there, fussing over the other patients. Maybe the Shriners had arrived to pass out little bottles of booze. He wanted to go!

"It's slackening," he said, his chin jutting forward stubbornly.

"No, it's not, Uncle Cees," Mrs. Little said.

"It sounds like it to me."

"Uncle C. C., I do not drive in the rain," she reminded him.

"I'll drive," Cassie offered.

"No."

Cassie kicked the wrapping paper again, this time like a two-year-old having a tantrum, with both feet, sending paper all over the floor.

"Cassie," Mrs. Little warned.

"Well, Roger will probably never want to see me again, and it's all because of those stupid guppies."

Jimmie sat on the sofa, idly turning through one volume of his encyclopedia. He had a contented feeling.

96

Part of it, he knew, was relief. He had realized something about Chicken Little that morning. Chicken Little was not the Peter Pan of his life, someone who would fly in at any moment, at any age, and turn him sick with fear. Chicken Little was a part of one summer, the summer after his father's death.

He could see that summer more clearly. He felt for the first time that there was a difference between the way he was then and the way he was now. One day he might be able to see this Christmas more clearly too.

The phone rang and Cassie went to answer it. In a moment she returned, smiling. "Mom, good news. Roger says he loves his guppies and he and I will drive Uncle C. C. back to the home."

Uncle C. C. was on his feet at once. He moved forward, his trembling hand already reaching for his cardboard suitcase. "I'm ready," he said firmly.

"Tell Roger I'd appreciate it," Mrs. Little said. There was genuine relief in her voice.

Mrs. Little had decided two days ago, in that dark moment when she had stalled the DeSoto on the hill and then had to pass the bread truck with her eyes closed, that she would give up driving once and for all. She had been worrying about the trip back to the home with Uncle C. C. She felt that one more drive would be pushing her luck, and she would hear, for the first time in her life, the sound she had always dreaded—the crash of fender against fender.

Uncle C. C. was struggling to put on his coat. His arm was caught in the lining of his sleeve. He muttered impatiently as he jammed his arm deeper into the lining. Cloth tore.

"I'll help you," Jimmie said as he got to his feet.

"Uncle Cees, it'll be at least ten minutes," Cassie said. "Roger has to warm up the car."

"I'm ready *now*."

Uncle C. C. stood like a bull, feet planted apart, chin jutting forward. His arms trembled slightly in his sleeves. He moved to the window to watch for Roger.

"Where *is* he?" he demanded.

"He'll be here, Uncle Cees."

Mrs. Little stood up, settling her Spanish shawl over her shoulders. She walked to Uncle C. C. and rebuttoned his coat, which, in his haste, he had done wrong.

"There." She patted his lapels fondly. "Now, you come back to see us real soon."

"From now on," Uncle C. C. said firmly, stepping back out of reach, "*you* come to see *me*."

"I'd like to do that," Jimmie said. "I could take the bus."

It seemed to him that he was becoming more like

his mother. Now that he had started liking his family, he really liked them. He valued Uncle C. C.

"Yes, you come," Uncle C. C. said, turning his small powerful eyes on Jimmie. "We can talk."

Jimmie nodded.

"You're—" Uncle C. C. paused. Then he paid Jimmie his highest compliment. "You're a good listener."

"Thank you."

"Here he is!" Cassie called.

"Good-bye," Uncle C. C. said quickly. He reached for the doorknob.

"Wait, the umbrella! Get it, Jimmie. Uncle Cees, wait for the umbrella."

"I can make it."

"No! Uncle Cees!"

"Get away from me!" He screeched like an owl. He saw now that Mrs. Little would do anything to prevent his leaving. He could not blame her for this, but he wanted to go.

He struggled with Mrs. Little, feebly pushing away her arms. The woman was an octopus, he thought. He batted at her many arms as if they were flies.

"Now, Uncle Cees, it'll only be a minute," she said soothingly. She came closer.

Uncle C. C. edged away from her, sideways like a crab. His old eyes were sly. He had a maneuver in mind—a fake to the left, a quick shift to the right and out the door. All her arms couldn't stop him.

While he was still going sideways she said, "See, here's Jimmie now."

Uncle C. C. sighed with relief. On the alert for any tricks, any attempt to detain him, he went down the steps with Jimmie behind him, holding the umbrella over his head.

He pulled himself into the backseat of the car, cursing modern cars which seemed no longer designed with him in mind. He attempted to pull the door shut himself. Jimmie reslammed it.

"Good-bye," Uncle C. C. said again. There in the backseat, safe at last, he drew his first easy breath of the day.

"Good-bye, Uncle Cees," Jimmie called through the window.

"Good-bye, good-bye, *good-bye*," he answered impatiently. He pushed down the button, locking his door, so no one could pull him back into the house.

Mrs. Little motioned to him to roll down the window, but he pretended he couldn't understand. He pointed to his ears, pantomiming deafness. "Let's go," he said to Roger.

Roger started the car and they drove away. Mrs. Little and Jimmie stood on the sidewalk, under the umbrella, watching. Jimmie waved as the car moved up the street. When it turned the corner, Mrs. Little and Jimmie started up the steps.

"It turned out to be a nice Christmas after all," Mrs. Little said. She drew her shawl up on her shoulders.

"Yes, it did," Jimmie agreed.

He shut the umbrella and shook off the rain, and they went into the house together.

AFTERWORD

Three weeks after Christmas the ice on the Monday River melted, and Uncle Pete's body was found downstream. There was a funeral, quiet and dignified, but it didn't seem to have anything to do with the Pete the family had known.

Instead, they all looked back, with happiness, to what they had come to speak of as Pete's party.

BETSY BYARS was born and grew up in North Carolina. She was graduated from Queens College, in Charlotte, and now lives with her professor husband in West Virginia. They are the parents of three daughters and a son.

Betsy Byars is the author of many books for children. Among them, THE SUMMER OF THE SWANS was awarded the Newbery Medal in 1971, and THE PINBALLS, which was an ALA Notable Book and received numerous honors, was the basis of a popular ABC *Afterschool Special.*